THE LAST DINOSAUR

by JIM MURPHY • Illustrated by MARK ALAN WEATHERBY

SCHOLASTIC INC.

New York Toronto London Auckland Sydney

*With special thanks to Dr. Paul Sereno, Assistant Professor,
Department of Anatomy from the University of Chicago,
for checking factual details in the text.*

ISBN 0-590-41098-9

Text copyright © 1988 by Jim Murphy.

Illustrations copyright © 1988 by Mark Alan Weatherby.

12 11 10 9 8 7 6 5 4 3 2   0 1 2 3 4 5/9
Printed in the U.S.A.   08

The Dinosaurs Disappear

FOR OVER 140 million years, dinosaurs ruled the world. They lived every-where: in the forests, near swamps and rivers, and on the open plains. So many dinosaurs were around that other types of animals found it hard to exist. For instance, only very small mammals could survive around the dino-saurs, and they spent their lives hiding under bushes or in tall trees.

Then suddenly the dinosaurs began to die off, and one kind after another disappeared forever. Why did this happen? Some scientists who study dinosaurs believe they were infected by a deadly disease. Others think a giant comet struck the earth, sending up a large cloud of dust that blocked the sun. This would have caused the temperature on earth to drop, and dinosaurs would not have been able to find food or survive the colder weather.

Probably a variety of reasons having to do with climate, food sources, and sickness ate away at dinosaur populations over a long period of time. Then something very unusual, such as the comet, finished them off. If the cause of "the great dying" remains unclear, the effect isn't. Areas that once had many of the creatures soon had only a few. This story will let you see what some of these last dinosaurs might have experienced. It opens at dawn, 65 million years ago, at the very end of the Age of Dinosaurs.

THE SUN came up slowly, fingers of light poking into and brightening the tangled forest of pine and poplar and hemlock trees. The drone of insects quieted, and the tiny mammals scampered to hide.

In a clearing a small Triceratops herd began their day. The female Triceratops blinked several times before moving to get the light out of her eyes. Then she went back to the frond she'd ripped from a cycadeoid.

The frond was tough and spiky, but her sharp-edged beak and rows of teeth chopped the plant into easily swallowed pieces. She was about to tug at another frond when a male Triceratops began stamping his feet in alarm.

He had been feeding at the base of a tree when his horns became entangled in a mass of grapevines. He shook his head violently to get free. When that didn't work, he backed away, yanking his head from side to side. Still covered with vines, he halted. His breathing came in short, grunting pants.

Suddenly he lowered his head and charged the tree. He hit it solidly, backed up, and hit it again, and then again. The fourth butt splintered the tree's base and it leaned over. A few wiggles of his head and the vine slipped off.

He snorted at the vine, challenging it. When it didn't move, he walked around it and left the clearing. He was the largest Triceratops and leader of the herd, so the smaller male and the female followed him.

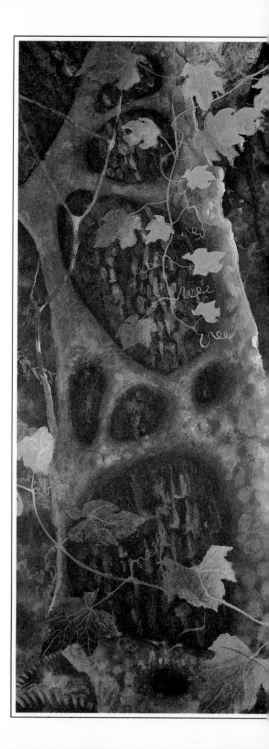

The three wandered through the forest, always staying near the stream that was their source of water. They did not hurry, and often stopped to nibble at figs or tender tree saplings. On the second day they came to a hillside covered with tasty ferns. The spot was cool and quiet, so they stayed the afternoon, browsing.

A sudden noise made the female jerk up her head to look and listen. They had not seen another dinosaur in a very long time, but she was still wary. A hungry Tyrannosaurus might have picked up their scent and followed, hoping one of them would stray from the herd.

The two males sensed her unease and also looked around. A giant dragonfly circled the Triceratops, then flew away. A bird chattered briefly. Then the forest grew still. Was a Tyrannosaurus out there, watching, waiting? Nothing moved and the noise did not return, but the herd was nervous. They left the hillside and continued their journey.

The next day, the land sloped downward and the stream widened to become a series of falls, pools, and swirling rapids. The path twisted to follow the water and dipped sharply in places. Despite their great size, the Triceratops walked the narrow ledges and leaped boulders with an easy grace.

The female Triceratops smelled something. Her sense of sight was very poor, so she turned to face what was causing the strange odor. Wisps of smoke trailed through the trees.

The smoke was from a fire started the night before by heat lightning. The female couldn't see the fire or know that it was advancing toward them. But the smoke was growing thicker and more unpleasant, so the three animals trotted away.

All night they moved quickly to stay clear of the smoke. At dawn, the ground leveled, and the smell seemed to disappear. The two males stopped, exhausted, and bent to drink the cool water. The female continued along the path.

Weeks before, the female Triceratops had mated with the leader of the herd. She was hunting now for a spot to build her nest.

The leader stamped his feet and snorted for her to stop, but it did no good. The female would not obey until the nest was completed and her eggs laid. This time, the males followed.

A mile downstream, the forest thinned and the stream emptied into a broad marsh. In the past, dome-headed Pachycephalosaurus or armored Ankylosaurus would be browsing in the cattails and rushes. Now only the bones of a long dead Anatosaurus, half buried in mud, were there to greet the herd.

The female walked the edge of the marsh carefully. The ground was either too wet or too rocky for the nest. On the opposite side of the marsh she found a warm, sandy area with low-growing shrubs.

Immediately she began digging, using the toes of her front and rear feet to shovel out the sand. The hole she dug was six feet across and a foot deep.

When the hole was finished, she laid fifteen eggs in it to form a circle. Gently she covered the eggs with sand. The sun would warm the sand and eggs, and eventually baby Triceratops would emerge.

The two males were feeding a little distance from the nest. The smaller male approached the nest.

When the female saw him, she placed herself between him and her eggs and lowered her head as a warning. The curious male kept coming, so the female charged him. Only when he backed away did the female stop her charge.

When the herd had been larger, many females would make nests in the same area. They would then take turns guarding the nests or feeding and sleeping. But the female Triceratops was alone now. It would be her job to keep clumsy males and egg-eating creatures away from her eggs. The quick shrewlike mammals were especially annoying at night.

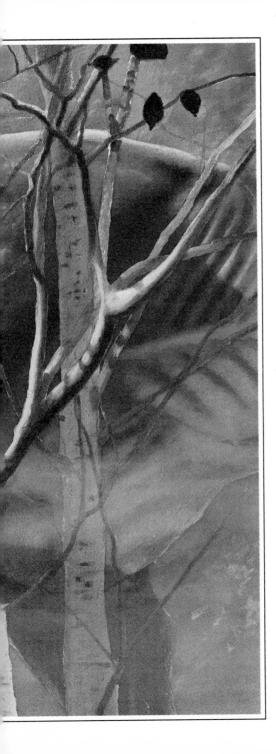

Two days later the smell of smoke returned. It was faint, distant, and yet the three Triceratops grew nervous. The female paced near her nest.

Late in the day, a heavy line of smoke appeared on the other side of the marsh. Flames erupted, reaching into the air.

A flock of birds flew overhead, screeching an alarm. Mammals, made bold by their fear, left their hiding places and ran from the fire. The two males edged away, but the female stayed to guard her eggs.

In the smoke and dark forest shadows, something moved. The shape was big, as big as many of the trees, and had a massive head. Tyrannosaurus rex. The giant flesh-eater stepped from the forest, snapping his mouth to reveal seven-inch-long slashing teeth.

Instinctively the two Triceratops males rejoined the female and formed a semicircle barrier in front of the nest. The leader lowered his head and stared at his enemy. Neither moved.

Ordinarily, the Tyrannosaurus would not attack a Triceratops, especially near its nest. But a wall of flames and heat had cut off his retreat. Besides, the Tyrannosaurus had not had a large meal in weeks.

The Tyrannosaurus darted at the herd, skidded to a sudden halt, then began circling warily, watching for a chance to strike. He hissed and snapped his teeth. At that instant, the largest Triceratops charged, his powerful legs driving him directly at the soft belly of his attacker.

With the aid of his long tail and thickly muscled legs, the Tyrannosaurus leaped aside to avoid the sharp horns. He spun and dove, mouth wide open, and sank his teeth into the back of the Triceratops.

Then the smaller Triceratops lunged at the giant, but he was an inexperienced fighter. The Tyrannosaurus' teeth closed on his neck and with a quick, deadly yank, he tore a chunk of flesh from the Triceratops. The smaller Triceratops fell, dying.

The other Triceratops tried to charge again, but his right leg was dragging and his movements were slow. Again the Tyrannosaurus moved aside easily. Using his tail as a spring, the Tyrannosaurus launched himself for the kill. His teeth sank into the Triceratops, while his clawed feet struck him in the stomach. The two rolled, kicking and biting each other.

At this moment, the female Triceratops abandoned her eggs and rammed the Tyrannosaurus full in the side. He bellowed painfully, releasing his hold on the male. The female pushed forward with all her strength, pinning the Tyrannosaurus against a tree and driving her horns in deeper.

She stepped away and watched her enemy, ready to charge if he got up. His legs and tail flailed weakly, his breathing became labored. Then, with a violent shudder, the great killer died.

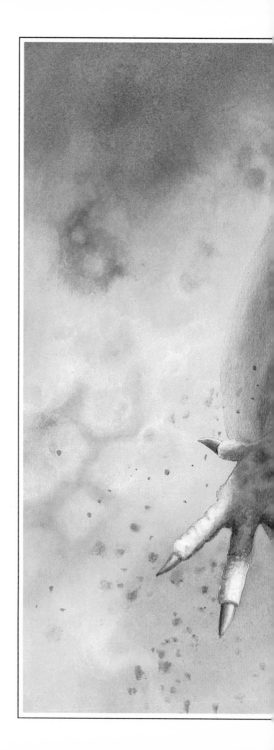

During the battle, the fire had spread, leaping and dancing from tree to tree until it reached the edge of the sandy area. Flames rolled through the reeds.

The male Triceratops struggled to get up, but his legs buckled under him. He crawled a few feet but had to stop. His wounds were too severe. A choking wave of smoke surrounded him.

The female Triceratops went back to protect her eggs. To one side a tree crashed to the ground, sending up an explosion of sparks. A bush nearby caught fire. The female charged it, slashing at it blindly with her horns.

The roar of the fire became deafening, and the heat and smoke grew painful. Reluctantly the female moved away from her eggs to find air.

She went only a short distance and turned to go back. The smoke stung her lungs and burned her eyes. She shook her head, but the choking pain would not go away. She backed away some more and lost sight of her nest.

Immediately the tiny mammals pounced on the unguarded nest. Low to the ground the smoke was not so thick. Digging hastily, they uncovered the eggs and devoured them. Then they scurried from the approaching fire.

The female Triceratops hurried through the forest. Several times she stopped to look back toward her eggs. A wall of smoke and flames was all she could see. Finally she gave up.

A tongue of flames reached out at her, and she broke into a gallop. She crashed through branches and vines, leaped over fallen logs heedlessly, with the fire just behind her. At last she came to a rock ledge overlooking a wide river.

The water was dark and deep. Branches and tree roots floated near the banks. The female wanted to find another retreat, but she was surrounded by flames. She hesitated a second, then jumped into the water.

Legs churning frantically, she swam across the river and away from the fire. The river's current caught her, pulling her swiftly along. She struggled to keep her head above water, to breathe, all the while moving her legs. At last her feet touched the river bottom.

Exhausted, her breathing fast, she hauled herself onto solid ground. Across from her, the fire had stopped at the river's edge. She was safe. It was then she noticed the streams of mammals that had also crossed the river to escape the fire.

The light grew dim and the air became chilly. The female's breath gave off thin vapor streams.

The Triceratops shook her head and snorted. She hadn't eaten much in days and wanted to find some tender plants. And maybe, somewhere deep in the forest, there was another Triceratops herd she could join.

Slowly, as the sun went down, the female pushed through the bushes to begin her search.

A Lucky Beginning

IT'S SAD to think about the death of the dinosaurs. But we shouldn't be too sad about their end. Our knowledge of them suggests they were amazing survivors, occupying every corner of the world and adapting to changing climates and food sources for millions of years. While knowing why they died off is important, we can probably learn a great deal more about the earth and how to exist on it successfully by studying the way dinosaurs *lived* day to day.

In fact, we shouldn't consider the death of the dinosaurs as an ending at all. If anything, we can think of it as a lucky beginning.

With the dinosaurs gone, scientists believe that the timid mammals found the world a much safer place. They came out from under their bushes, down from their treetop hiding places. In time their numbers increased, and they began to explore the world around them. The Age of Dinosaurs might have come to an end, but the Age of Mammals was just beginning.

TriceraFacts

CAN WE be absolutely sure that a Triceratops was the very last dinosaur? No, not really. Thousands of dinosaur fossils have been dug up and studied, but these represent only a small number of the dinosaurs that existed. Until the fossil record is complete, the honor of being "the last dinosaur" will be as much of a guess as why it died. Despite this, the Triceratops is still the best candidate.

The Triceratops was a huge, powerful animal. It could grow to thirty feet in length and weigh as much as twelve thousand pounds. Nearly one third of its body was a massive head that sported three long, sharp horns. If this was not enough, a Triceratops possessed amazing speed. One scientist estimates that a charging Triceratops could reach speeds of thirty miles per hour. Imagine having one of these coming at you!

Alone, a Triceratops was a remarkable fighter. But they rarely had to fight alone. Scientists believe they roamed in herds that could number fifty or more. Even the mighty Tyrannosaurus would shy away from a confrontation with a herd of angry Triceratops.

Another and maybe even more important reason for the long survival of the Triceratops was the design of its mouth. A Triceratops had a razor-sharp beak, rows of teeth, and giant jaw muscles. These let a Triceratops eat a wide variety of plants, even the thickest and most fibrous leaves and branches. There were many other plant-eating dinosaurs around, of course, but they ate only one or two specific plants. When those plants changed or died off, these other plant-eaters went hungry.

Looking at a picture of a Triceratops, we might think they were big, clumsy, funny-looking animals. They were certainly big and maybe they were funny-looking. But they were also highly efficient browsing animals who, if annoyed enough, could become ferocious, agile fighting machines. If any dinosaur had the ability to be "the last," it was the Triceratops.